Grandma and Granapa Love Their RV

Written and illustrated
by
Bernd and Susan Richter

Published by
Saddle Pal Creations, Cantwell, Alaska, USA

Acknowledgements:
We owe special thanks to Linda Thurston for her editing effort
and valuable suggestions and to Cantwell's "computer-wiz"
Dean Phillips for continued technical support.

To our Saddle Pals
Kasey & Scott

Designed, produced, published, and distributed in Alaska by:
Saddle Pal Creations, P.O. Box 175, Cantwell, AK 99729, USA

Other children's books by Bernd and Susan Richter available
through Saddle Pal Creations:

- When Grandma and Grandpa visited Alaska they ...
- When Grandma visited Alaska she ...
- Do Alaskans Live in Igloos?
- How Alaska got its Flag
- Uncover Alaska's Wonders (a lift-the-flap book)
- Peek-A-Boo Alaska (a lift-the-flap board book)
- Come along and ride the Alaska Train
- Alaska Animals - Where do they go at 40 below?
- Goodnight Alaska - Goodnight Little Bear (a board book)

www.alaskachildrensbooks.com

INTRODUCTION

Have you ever wondered why Grandma and Grandpa often leave home for weeks at a time in their Recreational Vehicle (RV) motor home or travel trailer? Well, Grandma and Grandpa worked hard all their lives and now that they have some extra time on their hands, they use it to enjoy some of their hobbies. And one of their favorite hobbies is traveling around the country and living in the great outdoors. Travel brings out their sense of discovery and adventure.

Does it make you sad when Grandma and Grandpa go on one of these trips? You know, Grandma and Grandpa would love to take you along. Unfortunately, most of the time they are gone for too long to have you miss school or be away from your family and friends.

If you wondered what you are missing, keep on reading and you will discover the magic of being on the road with Grandma and Grandpa.

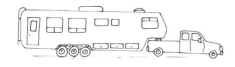

HAPPY TRAILS!

Today is the day Grandma and Grandpa have been looking forward to for some time now. It is the day they start getting their beloved RV ready for another vacation trip. Here we see them taking off the cover that protects the RV while it's parked in their backyard when it isn't being used. The RV is as big as a school bus and takes a lot of gasoline to operate. That is why Grandma and Grandpa don't drive it everyday when they are at home. They don't need a vehicle with its own bedroom, living room, kitchen, and bathroom just to go to the store. But for long road journeys the big RV is perfect!

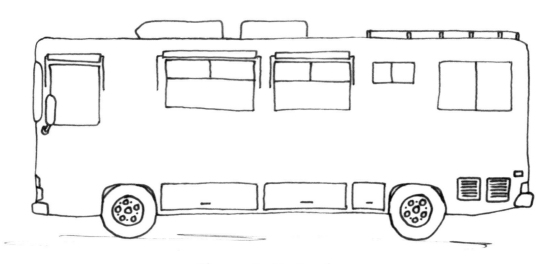

Class A Motorhome

Before they start their long road trip, Grandpa makes sure that the RV is in good working order. He checks the spark plugs, belts, hoses, fluid levels, brakes and everything else that makes an engine and the RV run safely.

While Grandpa is busy working on the engine, Grandma loads the RV with supplies they will need on the long trip. These include everything from food to cooking utensils, camping and fishing gear, towels, clothes for both warm and cold weather, computer, and hobby items such as sewing needles, yarn, whittling knives, and musical instruments.

All these chores keep Grandma and Grandpa busy for several days. But they enjoy the work because Grandma and Grandpa know that they are getting ready for adventure.

Class C Motorhome

The big day is here!

Grandma and Grandpa finish packing the RV, lock their house, and drive out of town ready to discover new places. As you can see, they are well prepared. They have brought bicycles, a boat, and even a second car.

Why tow a car behind the RV, you wonder? Well, the small car gets better gas mileage than the big RV. Grandpa just unhooks the car after they park the RV when they are staying someplace several days. Then Grandma and Grandpa drive the small car instead of the RV to save money on gas.

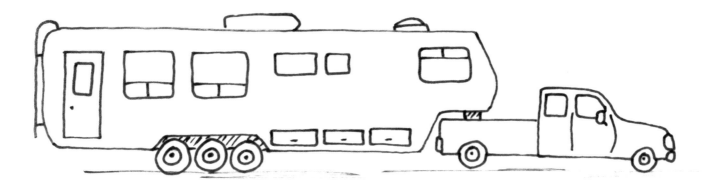

Heavy-duty Pick-up Truck with Fifth-wheeler

Grandma and Grandpa have spent weeks carefully planning their trip deciding where to go and what to see. Grandpa promises to show Grandma dangerous snakes. He knows just where to go and how to get there. Can you guess where they will go to see snakes?

Grandma says she wants to show Grandpa the faces of four famous men carved into a mountainside. The faces are so huge that each nose is as big as a pick-up truck. Grandpa says he will believe it when he sees it.

They also decided to return to the most famous national park in the world - Yellowstone. And they want to go to the Pacific Ocean, one of their most favorite places.

All of these destinations are marked on the road map that Grandma packed earlier. To make sure Grandpa doesn't take a wrong turn, Grandma studies the map. This way she and Grandpa will know how to find their way and how not to get lost.

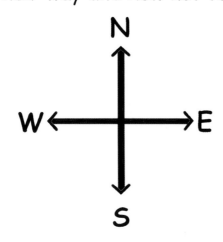

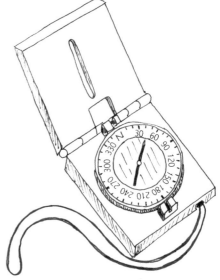

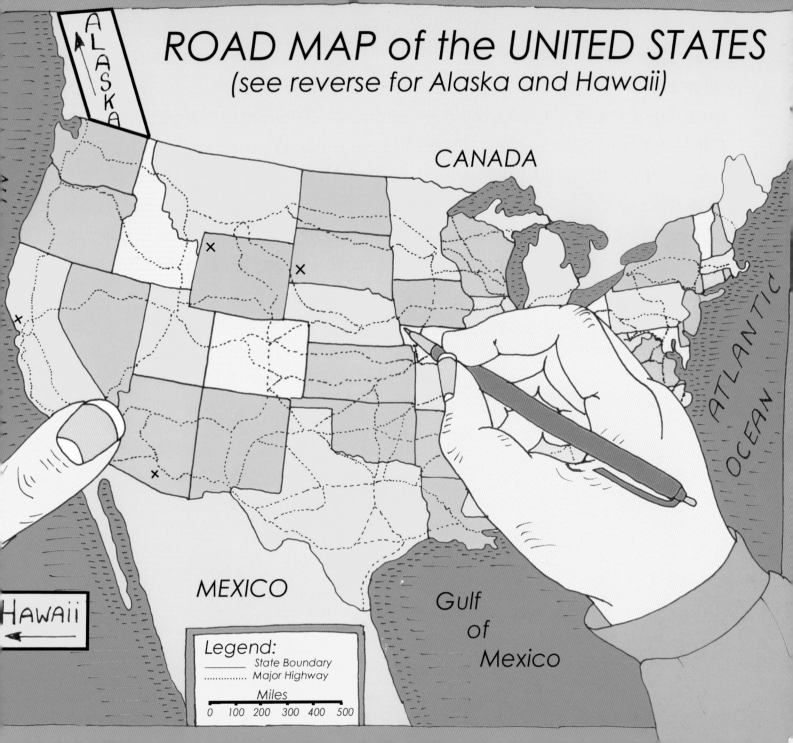

Some of the magic of travel for Grandma and Grandpa is the ever-changing scenery outside their RV windows. They pass through huge cities and tiny ghost towns, through green forests and pink and brown and red deserts, past prairie land so flat they can see for tens of miles ahead.

In this picture of hill country, Grandma and Grandpa don't know what to expect around the next curve in the road. What will they see? Do you think it will be snakes or perhaps four carved faces with noses 20 feet long? Not knowing but getting surprised again and again makes traveling so interesting and so much fun for them.

Diesel Truck Hauler with Fifth-wheeler

Most mountain scenery is created by nature when water, ice, and wind carve up steep mountainsides and broad valleys. But in the hills of South Dakota an enormous man-made monument is carved into the steep slopes of Mt. Rushmore. Looking out at us are the faces of four former U.S. presidents - George Washington, Thomas Jefferson, Theodore Roosevelt, and Abraham Lincoln.

These are the faces with the 20-feet long noses Grandma had wanted to see since she was a little girl. Can you guess how tall these faces might be? Each of them is 60 feet tall! Now Grandpa is a believer, and he and Grandma are so happy to see this spectacular piece of historic art.

Thomas Jefferson
3rd President
(1801-1809)

Theodore Roosevelt
26th President
(1901-1909)

George Washington
1st President
(1789-1797)

Abraham Lincoln
16th President
(1861-1865)

After the excitement of the day, it feels great to Grandma and Grandpa to pull into an RV park for the night. These parks are located all over the country and offer many comforts for tired travelers. Among them are shady parking areas with picnic tables and electrical hook-ups to run the RV's refrigerator and lights, TV, air conditioner and furnace. They also provide water hook-ups for the sinks, shower, and toilet. Sometimes the park even has a swimming pool to cool off and relax in. Do you think Grandma and Grandpa are pulling into an RV park with a swimming pool right now?

Awning

Slide-out
living room

Classs C Motorhome set up for camping

As a matter of fact, they have. And that's where Grandma and Grandpa head right after they park the RV. They can't wait to jump into the cool water and then stretch out in the sun. Best of all, they enjoy meeting other travelers at the pool. They all sit in the sun and "network," which is exchanging news about road conditions, other RV parks, campsites, and interesting places to visit in the area. Over the years, Grandma and Grandpa have made several life-long friends of people they have met along the road - another reason why they love traveling in their RV so much.

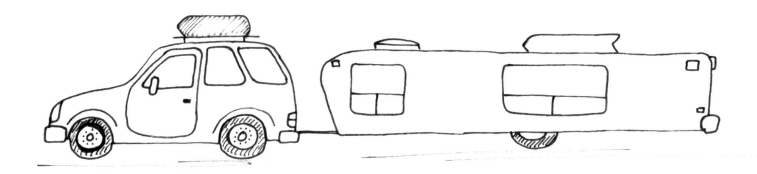

Sport-Utility-Vehicle (SUV) with pop-up camper trailer

After a busy day of sightseeing and swimming, Grandma and Grandpa are ready for a good night's sleep. They are so happy to have a comfortable bed in their RV. They remember back to when they were younger and often slept in a tent on an air mattress when camping with their young children - your mom or dad!
That was fun then, but nowadays they prefer to sleep in a real bed.

Pick-up Camper

After a great night of refreshing sleep, it is early to rise for Grandma and Grandpa. There is much to see and a full day of driving lies ahead of them. Grandma and Grandpa decide to join up with the new friends they met at the RV park. They will travel in what is known as an RV caravan, following one another along the roads and camping together at night. If they have car trouble along the way, they can help each other. Traveling with friends will be twice the fun.

They all drive up a long mountain pass in the Rocky Mountains. This is the largest mountain range in the U.S. Driving uphill is slow going for the heavy RV's, but that's okay with Grandma who enjoys the beautiful scenery and watches for animals and wildflowers along the road. Look at the graceful swans over there!

Caravan of RVs

Tonight, Grandma and Grandpa won't stay at an RV park but in a forest. Their RV is self-contained with a generator for electricity and big tanks for water. Grandma and Grandpa love that freedom of being able to stop and camp almost anywhere they want to. Tonight, they stay at a campground in the world's most famous park, Yellowstone National Park in Wyoming. Grandma and Grandpa love to stay in national parks and forests because there is so much to discover. Some of them have interesting animals, such as grizzly bears or crocodiles, while others have trees hundreds of feet tall. Some have enormous glaciers, while others have beautiful lakes for boating and fishing. Some have high mountains, while others have deep caves. Every park has something special and unique to offer, but all have one thing in common, that is, they are great places to enjoy the outdoors.

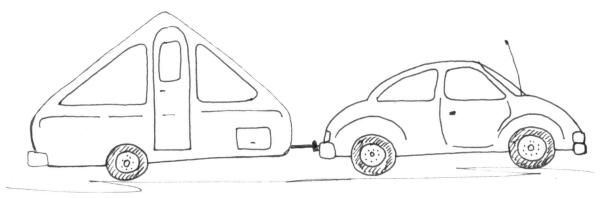

Passenger car with light-weight camping trailer

National parks are staffed by U.S. Park Service rangers, biologists, and interpreters who help take care of the parks' resources, animals, plants, rivers and lakes, campgrounds, and, of course, the visiting tourists. Answering questions and offering information about the parks for the public is a big part of the park service employees' duties. And learning about the natural wonders they visit is one of Grandma and Grandpa's favorite things to do. Sitting around the nightly campfire is especially fun when park employees tell stories and share interesting facts about the park and its wildlife, plants, rocks, and history.

Pop-up Camper Van

Last night Grandpa learned from the park biologist where to catch the best fish. So, early next morning Grandpa puts on his waders and gets out his fishing gear to catch a big one. Grandpa has fished ever since he was a little boy, and he has looked forward to this day of fishing for months. When he catches a big fish he will take it back to the campsite for dinner. But if he catches a little one he always releases the fish back into the water to give it a chance to grow bigger. Ask Grandpa what's the biggest fish he has ever caught.

While Grandpa tries his best to catch a big fish for dinner, Grandma drives the car to town. She calls home to talk to you and she does some shopping for that fish dinner. Grandma likes to buy fruits and vegetables directly from farmers because their products are always fresh out of the garden and flavorful. Grandma is famous for her cooking back home, and she still cooks up a storm in her RV kitchen.

Pineapple

Cherry

Grapes   Lettuce

Banana   Grapefruit

Peanut

Melon

Peach

Mushroom   Strawberry   Bell Pepper

Pear

Celery

Apple

Plum

Pumpkin

Lemon

Onion

Tomato

Carrot   Raspberry

Cucumber

Guess what! Grandpa caught his limit of fish. And he caught some of the best-tasting fish there are - cutthroat trout. This means he and Grandma will have people over to their campsite for dinner tonight. When Grandpa offers to share his big catch with fellow campers, he finds there is no shortage of volunteers. The guests bring food to share as well, which makes for a big potluck feast. But there is not just cooking and eating when friends meet. They also play cards, dominoes, music, or just trade travel stories.

Minivan with full-size camping trailer

Grandma and Grandpa have been to Yellowstone National Park many times before. Still, they visit this park whenever they have a chance because of its astounding natural beauty and wonders. Grandma and Grandpa can't get enough of those geysers, which spew hot water high into the air from deep below the land surface. The most famous geyser in the park is Old Faithful, gushing water 180 feet into the air. Grandma and Grandpa also like to watch the amazing mineral terraces, bubbling mud volcanoes, hot mineral springs, and waterfalls. This is truly a magical place. There are even buffalo and grizzly bears. But don't worry, Grandma and Grandpa keep a safe distance from these wild animals.

Mineral terrace   Geyser   Waterfall

Grandma and Grandpa love the outdoors whenever the weather is nice. When it rains, however, they enjoy some relaxation time inside their comfortable RV. This is a good time for Grandma to catch up on her travel journal and to write some postcards home to family, friends, and, most importantly, to her grandchildren. And come Sunday, Grandpa loves to sit in his easy chair and watch a ball game on TV.

Camper van with high-top roof

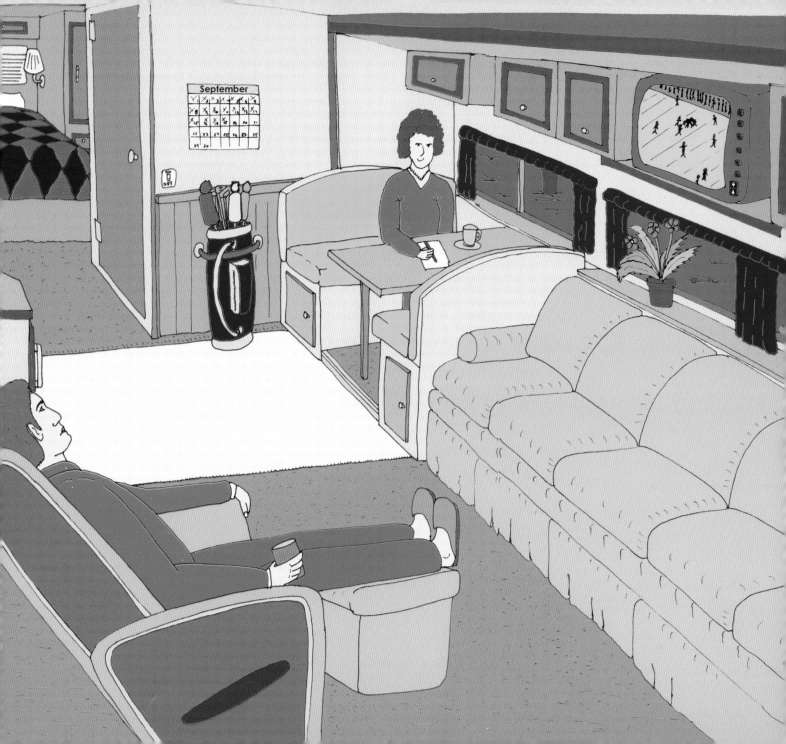

RV travel isn't all sightseeing and relaxing while on the road. When Grandma and Grandpa have been traveling for a while, they find that there comes a time when their clothes need to be washed. Fortunately, most RV parks offer laundry facilities with washing machines and clothes dryers.

Some RV parks are even set up to wash cars. Grandpa likes washing the vehicles whenever he has a chance because they get dirty quickly on gravel roads in the national parks and forests. He also checks the engine oil and the brakes on both vehicles again before heading out the next day. Safety is the number one priority for Grandma and Grandpa.

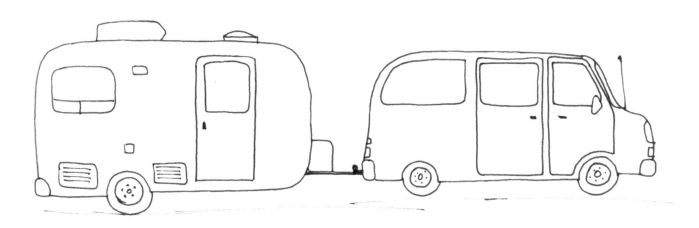

Minivan with medium-size camping trailer

After driving across the country, Grandma and Grandpa arrive at their major destination - the Pacific Ocean. They will stay here for a while, walking along the beaches, watching birds and sealife, fishing from their little boat, and relaxing in the sun. On a previous visit, they watched a pod of whales swim by and today they hope to see them again. Grandma and Grandpa also will go on a day trip to a sea lion rookery, which is not far from here.

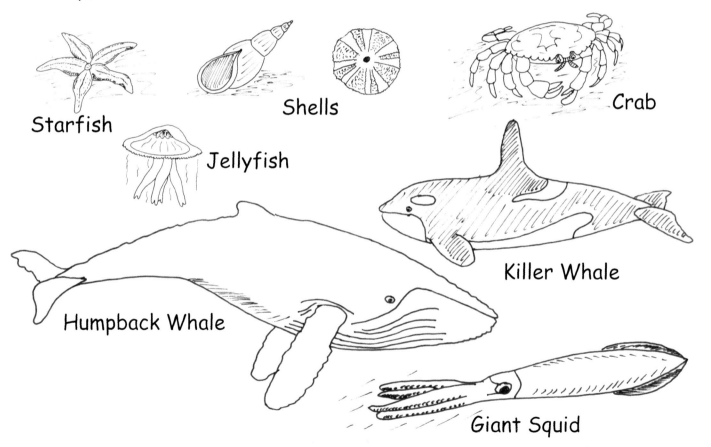

Starfish

Shells

Crab

Jellyfish

Killer Whale

Humpback Whale

Giant Squid

Just as a day ends with the setting sun, a vacation trip must eventually near its end. Here, Grandma and Grandpa gaze at a last spectacular sunset from their favorite beach. They will leave tomorrow to start their trip home. They wish they could take a little bit of beach and ocean home with them. They won't, of course, but Grandma and Grandpa know that they can always come back here again with their RV. Maybe they will bring you along next time.

Camper trailer with slide-out beds set up for camping

But the fun isn't over yet. Grandma and Grandpa take their time going home on a route different from the one they took before. This time Grandma and Grandpa drive through the Arizona desert where cacti grow to the size of trees. Grandpa has been looking forward to this part of the trip because now he can show Grandma the snakes he promised at the start of the trip. Can you find the dangerous rattlesnake in this picture? This desert is a very harsh environment for people, animals, and plants because of the heat and the scarcity of water. But it's also very pretty with its colorful rock formations and it's full of interesting history of the Wild West. Many movies about cowboys and Indians have been filmed in this desert.

Pop-up, pick-up camper

After being on the road and away from family and friends for such a long time, Grandma and Grandpa are happy to see their home and neighborhood again. They can't wait to tell family and friends about their great vacation. They will cherish the memories of this trip until they hit the road again for yet another adventure into the wonders of the world as seen from their RV. But that will be the subject of another book. For now we say:

Welcome back home, Grandma and Grandpa!

Your Travel Photos Here

Your Travel Notes Here

_____

_____

_____

_____

_____

_____

_____

_____

_____

_____

_____

_____

_____

Your Travel Photos Here

Your Travel Notes Here

Your Travel Photos Here

Your Travel Notes Here

_____

_____

_____

_____

_____

_____

_____

_____

_____

_____

_____

_____

Your Travel Photos Here

Your Travel Notes Here

_____

_____

_____

_____

_____

_____

_____

_____

_____

_____

_____